Olympus Rising

The Fallen, Volume 1

Robert G. Culp

Published by STEEL HOUSE PUBLISHING, 2021.

While every precaution has been taken in the preparation of this book, the publisher assumes no responsibility for errors or omissions, or for damages resulting from the use of the information contained herein.

OLYMPUS RISING

First edition. September 21, 2021.

ISBN: 979-8412803272

Written by Robert G. Culp.

Table of Contents

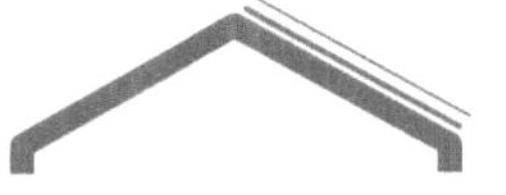

Chapter One
Arnold
Regal High

Arnold was suffering from another nightmare. Flashes of bloodshed and carnage filled his mind's eye. He was riding in a chariot pulled by winged boars as he led a Grecian army in ancient times. The battle seemed to go on forever, but Arnold finally reached his opponent — a man wearing a black cloak with silver armor and blades hidden underneath it. This man reeked of death and damnation. Arnold raised his axe and lunged at the cloaked figure, who moved just an inch of a second too fast and plunged a dagger into Arnold's chest. Gushes of golden blood poured from the wound. The cloaked figure laid Arnold down gently.

"...Why...?" Arnold managed.

"Because there was no other way..."

Arnold woke with a gasp as he saw his phone laying on his nightstand, had just gotten a text. He stood up and peaked out his bedroom window to see that the sun had risen. One nightmare might have ended, but another was just beginning.

"THERE'S NO WAY, MAN!"

A few hours later in the morning, Arnold and his best friend Hector Ramirez were riding their bikes to their first day at Regal High School.

"I'm telling you it's true," Arnold said as he took a shallow breath. He wasn't out of shape or anything; no, he was thin and lanky. Since they were nine, he and Hector had peddled these bikes to school every day. But as of this year, their old school, Wellington High, had finally been torn down due to lack of funds and a merger with the new head of the Regal City School Board. Meaning that now, Arnold and Hector had to pedal an extra five miles just to make it to another day of torture.

"No way could Hades beat an army of the gods," Hector said, wiping sweat off his brow. "I mean, the reason he got trapped in the underworld was because he couldn't beat his jackass brothers. So, how could he handle all the Olympians at once?"

"Speaking from experience, Hec?" Arnold let out a faint laugh.

"Who? Me?" Hector smirked as he shook his head. "Why do you think Xander's so good at track and field?"

"Hard work and dedication," Arnold said, in a deep voice, trying his best to mock the oldest Ramirez brother.

"Nah," Hector grinned. "It's because he's scared I'm going to catch up with him. And you know what would happen then...?"

"You'd spread your natural geekiness to him?" Arnold suggested.

"Well, duh!" Hector laughed. "That should go without saying; my geekiness is far too contagious. I've been suffering from it since I was seven."

"Dude, you've been around me since we were seven!" Arnold mocked in shock. "You infected me and that's why I'm a social reject?"

"Actually, I think you managed that all on your own," Hector laughed.

"Y'know," said Arnold, "I think that jackass problem runs in the family."

"You think?" Hector grinned. "Hey, we're only three blocks from school, and it's all downhill from there."

"Are you talking about the road or the rest of our lives?"

"The road, idiot," Hector chuckled. "I was going to suggest we race, but if you'd rather talk about your obvious existential crisis..."

"Oh, just shut up and race," Arnold laughed as they both took off like rockets down the hill.

"If you insist," Hector let out a shout of excitement as he then said, "by the way, the loser buys the winner cheeseburgers at CK after school!"

"You're on!" Arnold replied.

It was incredible how fast they were gliding downwards; Arnold didn't even have to pedal at all. He loved feeling the wind rush in his face; it made him wish he had a motorcycle instead of this cheap bicycle. He was edging in front of Hector and smiling like a madman. He could already taste his victory burger. Regal High was coming closer and closer into view; he was going to win. But then he heard Hector shout: "ARNOLD — CAR —!"

Arnold looked to his right on instinct and saw a yellow Camaro speeding his way. He was going too fast to stop, so he quickly made his bike take a turn to the left — where a bike rack was placed — but that hopefully wouldn't be a problem —

Arnold popped his bike up and jumped the rack — crashing instead into a picnic table that was part of the open grounds' cafeteria.

"Ares? Are you okay, my beloved?"

Arnold looked up hazily at a tall, beautiful blonde woman above him with sea-green eyes.

"Huh...?"

Arnold blinked twice and snapped back to reality. Emma Berggrias was kneeling by his side, offering a hand to help him up to his feet. Emma was petite but built with bulging muscles and had a mess of long flaming-red-hair. Though she did still have sea-green eyes.

"Thanks," Arnold mumbled embarrassedly, his cheeks going bright red. "I seriously need to learn how to stop."

Emma smiled. "Well, uh, yeah, that's pretty obvious. Don't tell me you and Hec were racing each other again."

"I would... but that would be a lie." Arnold gave her a sheepish half-grin.

"You know you're going to get yourselves killed one day, right?"

"Fully noted," Arnold shrugged.

"Thank the Divine; your mom didn't let you actually try to get a motorcycle license."

"...What?" Arnold blinked again.

"I said: Thank goodness, your mom didn't let you try to get a motorcycle license. ...Why? What did you think I said?" Emma cut her eyes at Arnold.

"Uh, nothing," said Arnold. "I've just been working on the graphics too much for the role-playing VR I've been designing."

"Mayhem On Mount Olympus?" Emma asked.

"Yeah," said Arnold. "You remembered?"

"It's only been one summer that I've been away," Emma chuckled. "Of course, I remember your passion project! You're practically like my brother!"

She playfully slugged Arnold's shoulder. He's her brother now? Like her little and completely unattractive brother. Great. Arnold was hoping things would be different this year. That things would change between him and Emma, but it looks like he was wrong, though. What did he expect? He was still the same as he had always been; same black, wavy hair, same scar on his bottom lip, and same non-muscular noodle arms. There was no way that Emma would ever see him as anything else. After all, they had grown up next door to each other, alongside Hector. The difference was Emma's family was rich, and Arnold and Hector's weren't. Emma's sister drove a Mustang Convertible and their family had spent the summer in Greece. Arnold had spent his summer in his mom's basement designing video games with whatever spare tech that people had carelessly thrown away.

"Hey — Regan!"

Arnold suppressed a moan as he and Emma turned around to see Helena Vivane strutting towards them, her iced mocha splattered all over her two-hundred-dollar blouse. "Look what you did!"

"Look, Helena," sighed Arnold, "I'm sorry. But it was either get run over by Henry's Camaro or crash into the picnic table. So, I took the lesser evil; I thought it would hurt less."

"You are such a waste of space!" Helena screeched. "You should have let Harry run you over and end your pathetic life! No one even cares about a little shit like you!"

"Hey, Helena."

"What?"

"Oh... just this!"

Emma slugged the crap out of Helena and then tackled her to the ground, pummeling every square inch of her face. Hector ran over to them. "What the hell? Oh, that's right. It's the first Monday of the school year, so of course, Emma's beating the shit out of someone."

"Hector — come on and help me pry her off Helena," said Arnold anxiously.

"Oh, so that's who she's thrashing," Hector mused. "I should have recognized her solid gold pumps. Finally, someone who deserves it."

"It doesn't matter if she deserves it or not," Arnold said in exasperation. "If the Principal or the teachers see her doing this..."

"Fine," Hector sighed. "But she better not kick me in the balls again, like last time."

The two boys grabbed each of Emma's swinging arms and yanked her off the bloody and bruised Helena.

"Let — go — of — ME!" Emma screamed the last part out. "I'M GOING TO DEMOLISH THAT BITCH!"

"Regan! Ramirez! Berggrias! Vivane! What on earth are you kids doing?"

Principal Gia had just walked out of the school and was giving each of them a death glare.

"Oh, ...son of a bitch," Arnold muttered underneath his breath.

Principal Gia gave all four of them a month's detention for the fight. By the time they all left her office, Emma's fraternal twin sister, Allison, was waiting for her. Allison was cute, usually perky, blonde, and the popular one.

"Emma — what in the hell did you think you were doing?"

"Oh, great," Emma rolled her eyes, "another lecture. How about you just record the podcast episode of this and play it to me later? I've been having trouble getting to sleep, anyway."

"Emma, don't you dare make insults about my podcast!" Allison lectured. "You know you enjoy them!"

"Oh, yes," Emma sighed. "They're just so riveting."

"Yes, they are," Allison nodded, not catching Emma's sarcastic tone. "Why did you get into a fight on our first day here?"

"Why didn't you?" Emma smirked.

"That's it!" said Allison. "I'm telling Mom that you need to go back to anger management therapy!"

"Yeah, sure," Emma pushed her hair out of her face, "because Principal Gia didn't even think to do that herself."

"Allison, it wasn't Emma's fault," Arnold tried to explain. "It was mine. I..."

"No," said Emma plainly, "it was mine. I'm just sorry I didn't bust Helena's lip along with her nose; that girl is such a snobbish bitch."

AS THE DAY WENT ON, it was mostly the same crap as it had always been at their old school. Boring classes, blah blah, mean teachers blah blah, and Henry Wheeler asking Arnold for Emma's number. Which Arnold told him she recently changed by... uh... mistake?

After school was their first detention, which lasted an hour. Afterwards, Helena, sporting several bandages over her nose, got a ride with Hector's brother, Xander. And Emma left begrudgingly with Allison in her Mustang. Leaving just Arnold and Hector to get on their bikes as a striking girl, their classmate, Pria Gluven, approached them.

"Hi, you're Hector Ramirez, right?"

Hector smiled at her in shock and awe. "I'm anyone you want me to be! But, uh, yeah. I'm Hicky — I mean — Hector. That's, uh, me!"

"I just want to tell you that I thought you were so brave and considerate to try and keep your friends from getting in trouble," said Pria. "And... maybe, if you're free now... you might like to go get a pizza or something? With — uh — me, that is."

Hector beamed at her and shot Arnold a pleading look. They were supposed to go get their cheeseburgers, but Arnold gave him an encouraging grin. Hector had been crushing on Pria for two years but could never find the courage to ask her out; he needed this. Hector turned back to Pria, smiled, and said: "I'd love to get a nibble on you — I mean, get a nibble with you! I — uh — do you like mushroom and jalapeño pizza?"

"I love mushroom and jalapeño pizza!" said Pria, mounting her bike as Hector did the same, and soon, the two were pedaling away together. Arnold shook his head, laughing as he got on his bike and pedaled up the hill.

ARNOLD HAD JUST REACHED the edge of the Regal City Dump. He was scavenging for any unused tech part to use in his game. He cursed a few times, as he couldn't seem to find anything that could help his work. He was about to examine an old 2012 Mac desktop interface when the entire dump shook savagely.

Is this some kind of freakin' earthquake? Arnold thought anxiously. *Regal City hasn't had one in over twenty years!*

But in seconds, three enormous beasts with black, scaly skin, red eyes, horns, the build of a giant dog, with large yellow and razor-sharp fangs, lunged at him. Arnold took off running, leaving the Mac behind.

Well, at least, now I know it wasn't an earthquake! Just literal demon-junkyard-dogs who want to make me their chew toy! That's soooo much better!

Arnold almost made it to the exit gate as he tripped and fell on his face as all three demon-dogs surrounded him. "Oh, shit. Shit! Shit!" Arnold cringed as one dog bit his ankle. But then — two cloaked figures tackled the attacking demon-dog and stabbed it with their bronze swords. The monster burst into flames with a howl.

The two figures each attacked the remaining demon-dogs, doing the same as they did with the first. Arnold struggled and failed to stand up as the two cloaked figures removed their hoods that were attached to their cloaks.

One was a tall, muscular man with blonde hair and sea-green eyes. He looked to be in his twenties. The other was a girl with dark hair, burning red eyes, and pale skin. She looked to be only eighteen at the most. The girl smiled at Arnold and ran over, hugging him tightly.

"We finally found you," said the girl happily. "Oh, Father, how I missed you!"

"...Father?" Arnold managed to get out. "I — I think you have the wrong guy. I'm only sixteen if you haven't noticed. So..."

"Oh, no," said the girl, waving it off. "That's just part of the curse of reality being reborn and all."

"Huh?" Arnold asked in disbelief.

"Yeah," said the girl. "You're Ares! The God of War! I'm Amelia, your godly daughter and that's my brother Tristan. And I hate to rush things, but we need to find Mom. Y'know? Aphrodite? Well, you call her Emma in this reality, but —!"

Tristan shook his head in impatience. "Digest version, sis."

"Oh, okay," said Amelia. "We're here to help all you reclaim your memories and godly titles before the Twilight of the Gods happens. Easy, right?"

"Right."

"Really?"

"No!" Arnold shouted. "You two are nuts! I'm not a god! Gods aren't even real!"

"Okay... well, how do you explain that then?"

Amelia pointed at Arnold's ankle where the demon-dog had sunk its fangs into him. He was bleeding... golden blood?

"Holy..."

Tristan smirked. "Father, you don't remember the meaning of the word."

Chapter Two
Arnold
Everything Is... Fine

Arnold had a lot to think about as he pushed his bike home. His ankle had already healed, for one thing. Plus, there was the fact that there were two almost grown adults carrying bronze swords who claimed to be his children. He tried to shake their conversation out of his head, but was failing miserably.

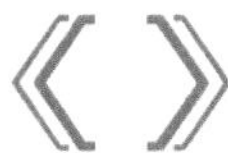

"WHAT THE HELL DID THAT demon-dog do to me?"

"It's okay, Father," Amelia had said. "All he did was bite you. And look — your wound is already healing!"

"He did more than bite him," sighed Tristan. "He kick-started your Olympian abilities. Soon, you'll almost be at half-strength."

"No," Arnold had said as his voice quivered. "No. No. No! You're crazy! All of this is crazy! There are no such things as Olympian Gods!"

"Why do you keep saying that?" Amelia asked.

"Because... if there were... the world wouldn't be so screwed up!"

"What have you suffered through?"

Amelia's words, paired with her look of concern, cut through Arnold's heart as if she had used one of her blades.

"Nothing!" Arnold shouted. "Look, it's none of your business! My life is fine! Or at least it was before you two came into it! Just — just leave me alone!"

YEAH. HIS LIFE WAS fine. Just as it had always been. *"OH, WAY DOWN WE GO!"* Shit! Arnold's phone was blaring one of his favorite songs, which meant he was getting a call from his mom.

"Hey, Mom. Sorry, I'm running late. ...Yeah, I'm okay. Oh? School? It was wonderful; Hector and I had a great time. ...Uh, yeah, Emma and Allison did, too. ...Sure, I'll pick up your prescription. It's no problem. I'm right near Walmart. I'll see you in a little while. ...I love you too, Mom."

Arnold ended the call and sighed. At least he didn't lie to his mom about everything. He was walking right by Walmart when she called. Arnold pushed his bike to the curb and chained it to a fire hydrant. He then walked, his shoulders hunched, into the parking lot.

He had just about made it to the entrance when he heard someone familiar shout out his name:

"Yo — Regan!"

It was Henry Wheeler. He was sitting on the hood of his Camaro alongside Pat Ramirez (Hector's other older brother) and Alaric Richardson. All three were Regal High's star football players. A game that Arnold refused to understand based on principle.

"What do you need, Henry?" Arnold sighed.

"I wanted to ask you if you could talk to Emma about going out with me on Saturday," Henry flashed his perfect smile.

"Sorry," said Arnold. "But I don't think you're her type."

"Why?" Henry asked. "She's fast, isn't she?"

"What did you just say?" Arnold snarled.

"I heard she puts out really nice if you know how to handle her," Henry smirked.

"Take that back, now!" Arnold said, his eyes flaring.

"Ooh, is little Arnold Regan going to fight me?" Henry chuckled. "I'm quaking in my boots."

"Hey, let's take a breather," said Pat, coming in between them.

"Come on, Pat," Henry grinned. "We're just having fun."

"I don't see it that way," said Pat calmly. "You've had too much to drink, Hank. So, go cool off with Alaric. While, I make sure that my baby brother's best friend doesn't get the shit knocked out of him, okay?"

"Whatever you say." Henry threw his hands up in the air and strutted back over to Alaric.

Pat grabbed Arnold's shoulder and steered him into Walmart. As soon as they were a good way inside, the younger teen broke free and glared at him.

"You didn't have to do that."

"What?" Pat rolled his eyes. "Save your life?"

"Try to help me because I'm friends with Hector," Arnold sighed.

"Is that why you think I did it?"

"What else could it be?"

"Maybe it's that your mom helped raise me and my brothers," said Pat. "And I don't want her actual son getting killed while she's..."

"Yeah, uh-huh," Arnold said half-heartedly. "Thanks, by the way, but you didn't..."

Arnold turned away from Pat and started to walk away. "Didn't what?" He heard Pat say.

"...save my life."

ARNOLD GAVE A GREAT sigh of relief once the prescription was in his hands. He'd made it to the pharmacy on time and was about ready to leave when...

"Arnold?" Emma was walking nearby, carrying a similar pharmacy bag. She looked pleasantly surprised. "I didn't think I would see you here this late. What's up?"

"I had to get Mom's prescription before they closed," Arnold smiled.

"You were out late at the dump again, weren't you?" Emma grinned.

"Yeah."

"Find any good tech this time?"

"Nope," said Arnold. "It was almost like ancient times back there."

"Y'know, I could always give you one of my old tablets or laptops?" Emma said kindly. "Y'know, ... if you wanted me to."

"Nah," said Arnold plainly. "I need to get that kind of stuff my own way. I mean, it's wonderful of you to offer, but..."

"You don't want a handout or any type of charity?" Emma asked, her eyebrows arched.

"Well, ... kind of... but... yeah," Arnold sighed.

"I can respect that," Emma shrugged. "But it's not a weakness to accept help when you need it, Arnold; just remember that, alright?"

"Sure," Arnold blushed despite himself. "Y'know... that jock Henry Wheeler's into you. He kept pestering me for your number or for me to introduce you."

"Oh?" Emma eyed Arnold cautiously.

"Uh, yeah," said Arnold. "He said there's this rumor going around that... that... that you're..."

"That I've slept with every guy at school?" Emma sighed. "Yeah. I'd heard about that too. Found out about it after I got sixteen text messages asking which I preferred: bathrooms or hotel rooms."

"Oh, god," Arnold said in disgust. "That's awful!"

"Oh, wait until you hear this," said Emma. "This one guy told me I should join the Vatican to repent for my sins. And then I got twelve new texts asking me if that's why my parents took me to Greece and Rome for the summer."

"That sucks!"

"Well, apparently I do, if the rumors have anything to say about it," Emma sighed. "You know who started all of this, right?"

"Helena?"

"Got it in one," said Emma. "Which, in a way, I should take it as a compliment."

"How so?" Arnold asked.

"I must have really caused a lot of expensive damage to her million-dollar nose job," Emma laughed. "If she's spread so many rumors in such little time."

"Probably," Arnold chuckled. "You can throw one hell of a punch."

"Good," Emma beamed. "Spread the word."

Emma and Arnold had just walked out of the Walmart exit as they heard Henry Wheeler come running towards them.

"Hank — please don't do this!" Pat shouted. But it came too late as a drunk Henry pushed Emma against the wall of the store and started groping her breast.

"Just give me a taste. I'll get down on my knees if you like."

Emma readied her fist: "GET OFF —!"

"— HER!" Arnold tackled Henry to the ground and slugged him repeatedly until he grabbed his wrists and threw the former backwards into the air. Arnold did a perfect flip and landed on his feet. Emma and Pat both stared at him in shock. Henry stood up and glared at Arnold. "What's this?" Henry picked up the prescription Arnold had gotten for his mom. *Damn't! Why did I drop those?* Arnold thought as he groaned in frustration.

Henry ripped the bag open and eyed the bottle of pills. "Take three pills twice a day to relieve pain? Well, that's going to be a little difficult..."

Henry opened the bottle of pills and started emptying them all into a nearby gutter.

"NO!" Arnold screamed. "YOU SORRY SON OF A BITCH!"

Arnold charged at Henry, giving him a series of nerve punches that would temporarily paralyze his arms. How Arnold knew to do this, he wasn't sure. He had never studied or practiced anything like this before. He had never even been in a fight until now. Arnold punched Henry's ribs and his eyes. Henry tried to kick Arnold off him, but Arnold caught his leg and tossed the jock five feet away. Arnold looked as if he was ready to kill someone as he started hyperventilating. He looked down at his mom's empty pill bottle. What was he going to tell her? She needed those desperately! He then looked at Emma, who was approaching him gently.

"Arnold... it's okay," she said quietly. "Everything's going to be fine."

Arnold's heart felt as if it was being torn in two. One part felt like it wanted to keep beating faster, accelerating with every breath, while the other wanted to calm down, so he wouldn't scare Emma.

"OH, GOD!" Arnold punched Henry's yellow Camaro with such brute force that the driver's door now had a dent in the shape of his fist. Arnold's heart started to go back to normal as he looked at a clearly freaked Emma.

"I — I'm sorry!" Arnold took off at a run, ripping his bike right off the chains, pedaling away as fast as he could.

He could hear Emma yelling: "ARNOLD — WAIT!" And Pat saying to Henry: "Still having fun, dumbass?"

WHEN ARNOLD WALKED up to his mom's bedroom that night, he did so with great trepidation.

"Arnold! It is so good to finally see you," his mom beamed when he entered.

"I'm happy to see you too, Mom," Arnold tried his best at a smile.

"Did you get my rheumatoid prescription?" she asked kindly.

"Uh... they were out of them today," Arnold lied. "But they should have more in soon, though. That's why I was there so long; I had them check in the back to see if there were any extras in stock they might have overlooked."

"That's my sweet boy," his mother replied. "Now, why don't you sit down with me a while, and we can watch a new Revelation of Warlocks."

"I will in a moment, Mom," said Arnold. "I have to go heat us up some leftovers first."

"Alright, just be careful."

"I will," said Arnold. "I promise."

"...Arnold?"

"Yes, Mom?"

"Is everything okay? You seem a little down."

"Everything is... fine."

After they ate and watched her favorite show, Arnold said goodnight to his mom. He then went down to the basement, or, as he called it, his workshop. He did his homework but fell asleep before he could advance anymore on his gaming software.

ARNOLD DREAMED HE WAS *inside a giant throne room where the beautiful blonde with Emma's eyes paced in circles.*

"We should have vouched for him, Ares! He was our best friend!"

"It's too late for that now, beloved," Arnold replied, deep in thought. "Hephaestus has sown his destiny and ours with it. You heard Athena at the trial. The world is changing far too fast. Twilight is coming."

"And what of our children?" said the blonde. "What if he comes for them too?"

"If he comes for our blood," said Arnold, "then I will slaughter him and his followers."

"And if you can't," said the blonde.

"Then, I will gladly lay down my immortal life for our children... and you... my sweet Aphrodite."

AS ARNOLD WALKED OUT of his house, trying to shake the feeling of dread his nightmares had left him, and locked his front door, he saw Amelia standing on his front porch.

"Hello, Father."

"Please, don't call me that," Arnold sighed.

"I'm sorry," she said sheepishly. "I just wanted to give you this." She took the 2012 Mac desktop interface out of her backpack and handed it to Arnold. "Uh, thanks," Arnold shrugged and sat the interface on his porch swing.

"I just wanted to let you know, I understand how hard it is to believe that any of this can be real," said Amelia. "For years, you and Mom hid me in different time periods, so your enemies couldn't find me. At times, I'd either forget who I was or think that I was going crazy. But then my powers would activate, and I would lose control and hurt people... people I had grown to care about. Until Tristan found me. Just know if you ever need anyone to talk to, whether you believe me or not, I'm here for you."

She turned to walk away as Arnold thought hard for a moment and then said: "I've been telling myself that everything has been fine for as long as I can remember... and for the past few months, that's been the biggest lie of my life. My mom has crippling rheumatoid arthritis, so I've been having to juggle taking care of her with everything else. And we're only barely surviving through her disability check. I've also been having nightmares of Ancient Greece, Mount Olympus, Aphrodite, Hephaestus, and who, I think, is Hades killing me. I thought at first it was because I was obsessing over my game design, but... I don't know whether you're telling me the truth... either way, though; I need answers. So, meet me after school at CK, and I'll hear you out, okay?"

"Thank you."

"For what?"

"Trusting me enough to give me a fair chance," Amelia smiled. "I'll see you soon, Fa — Arnold."

Arnold stared quizzically at Amelia as he watched her walk away gracefully. He then saw Hector run over to him from next door.

"Hey, man!" Hector said anxiously. "I just heard about what happened last night. ...Who's that?"

"Someone I haven't figured out yet," said Arnold casually. "But I'm going to..."

Chapter Three
Emma
To Love Is Pain

"**E**mma! It's time for school! I'm not going to be late... again!"

Emma groaned as she kept practicing her pull-ups. Allison was always annoying, but now she was absolutely driving Emma crazy.

"One-hundred and twenty-eight..."

Emma counted off with each successful pull. She usually wouldn't care if she was late for school. It had been a living hell recently (*thanks a lot, Helena!*), but she wanted to get there at a decent time. If for anything, to check on Arnold. He acted really strange the previous night. Arnold had always been so sweet and kind, but he fought like an angry pro during that fight. Usually, it was Emma who displayed that type of rage. He seemed so freaked out about all of it and some moves he used against Henry... well, even Emma didn't know how to do them, and she had been training as a fighter for six years now. Her father was the heavyweight kickboxing champ, after all. She had a lot to live up to, and she was never one to give up on a challenge. She loved to fight. There weren't really words on how to describe it better.

But Arnold? He always acted like a meek, little kitten. And she could have sworn she saw his eyes glow dark red for a second. Did it scare her? Not really. Emma had bipolar disorder, so she could understand having anger issues. Though she still couldn't understand how he could leave a dent in Henry's Camaro without breaking his hand...

"Emma?"

Ellie, Emma's little sister, had entered her room. "Allison says to tell you she's about to have a stroke if you don't come down in a few minutes."

"I should be so lucky," Emma muttered as Ellie giggled. "Mom really picked a perfect day to go awol. It's both of their faults. I have to take those damn meds again. They knock me out senseless, no matter what time I take them at night, which makes it a pain in the ass to wake up on Allison's perfect schedule."

"I think that it's the school's schedule, actually," said Ellie thoughtfully, pushing her horned-rim glasses back up her nose.

"...One-hundred and thirty," Emma sighed as she dropped herself down from the bar-mounted to her bedroom wall. "Regal High's a joke, sis." Emma grabbed a towel laying on her dresser and wiped the sweat from her brow. "Just a bunch of rich losers pretending to be something they're not."

"Even Arnie and Hec?" Ellie asked quietly.

"No, not them," Emma gave a small grin. "They're about the only people who really are comfortable in their own skin... most of the time."

"You know Mom and Allison just want you to take those pills because they're worried about you, right?"

Emma looked at Ellie sweetly. Her younger sister was thirteen and had the same red hair as Emma; only styled in tight braids. Freckles lined her naïve face. She needed to grow up... but Emma refused to be the one who made her do so.

"Sure, sis. I know."

Emma threw on her favorite faded t-shirt over her sports bra, along with a white-jean jacket. She was still wearing her yoga pants and sneakers, too. She grabbed her backpack, pausing to stare at the clearly ripped apart chains inside. Likewise, she shook off an eerie feeling and grabbed her iPhone. When she passed Ellie, she ruffled her hair as the latter cringed and scrunched her nose. "Don't you want to take a shower before you go? You're kind of stinking up the house."

"Then, you should be happy that I'm going to be spreading my stink all over Regal High and not here," Emma laughed. "Don't worry, it should all be gone by the time I get back."

"Really...?" Ellie raised her eyebrow.

"Maybe... or maybe not," Emma smirked. "We'll both find out tonight, though."

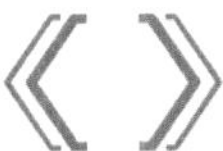

EMMA HAD TO LISTEN to Allison lecture her repeatedly about the positives and negatives of punctuality for the entire ride over to Regal High. She seriously needed to get her own car. During the lecture marathon, Emma drifted off into a deep sleep...

EMMA DREAMED SHE WAS walking inside a large, dark tunnel. It had many spiraling staircases leading in various directions. She held her white dress up with her hand, so her sandal-covered feet wouldn't trip on the hem, while her other hand carried a brightly lit torch. Soon, she finally reached her destination.

She knocked on a large, brass, mechanical door as it swung open automatically. She hesitated, but then entered cautiously. When her eyes met the sight of her beloved suspended in bronze shackles, her heart sank.

"Ares! What did he do to you?" She went to rush to the God of War's aid, but an invisible barrier stopped her. "...Grecian Powder."

"An excellent deduction, my love." Came a raspy voice from the shadows. It was Hephaestus. The battle-scarred and disfigured God of Forges and Fire. He was wearing brass armor that matched his door and various other inventions while carrying a large hammer he called Oxen. "Tell me, did you ever shed a tear when it was I who was imprisoned? Or did you not feel any guilt at all?"

"Hephaestus," Emma said as calmly as she could. "It doesn't have to be this way. What Ares and I did was wrong; we should have trusted your word instead of Hades."

"But you didn't," said Hephaestus, smacking his lips as he spoke. "Neither of you did! My best friend and brother! And the only goddess I ever loved! You let me suffer in Tartarus — FOR A CENTURY!"

Emma gave another heartbreaking look at Ares, who was barely fading in and out of consciousness. His beaten and stabbed body had golden ichor pouring from every wound. He was dying.

"You found the Deicide?"

"Aye," Hephaestus chuckled. "That I did. The one substance that can kill a god or immortal. What do you think dear old Oxen is

made from? Certainly not brass. If you don't get Ares back to Olympus for Apollo to heal, there'll be one more vacancy to fill on the Mountain."

"What do you want?" Emma asked him.

"Your hand in marriage," Hephaestus licked his lips.

"If I do so," said Emma as tears ran down her face, "will you call Hermès and allow him to bring Ares to Apollo?'

"Aye, I will," Hephaestus chuckled maliciously. "Do we have a bargain?"

"Yes," said Emma tearfully, "we do."

"Aphrodite... no... don't do this... please..." Ares begged. "Let me die... instead of living a life... without you..."

"I'm sorry, my beloved," Emma said in agony. "But love is pain... and I love you too much to lose you to death. This is the only way..."

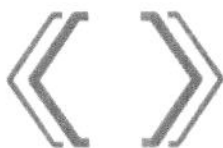

"EMMA, WE'RE HERE."

Emma forced herself to open her eyes and tried to force the tiredness in her body away. Allison was looking at her worriedly. Emma rolled her eyes and stepped out of the Mustang. She eyed the school parking lot, looking for her target of choice, ignoring Allison's concerned questions until she found him.

Henry Wheeler was walking into the empty metal shop classroom. Emma snuck in and locked the door behind them. Henry snapped around quickly as Emma snickered at his appearance. His swollen eyes black, and his leg had a visible bandage wrapped around it, right underneath the end of his shorts.

"What do you want?" He glared at her.

"I want you to leave Arnold and me alone," said Emma, firmly.

"You think I want any more of that asshole's crazy?" Henry asked, shaking his head in disbelief.

"Look, Arnold doesn't live in a world with rich daddies and their holier than thou lawyers. But I do. So, can you honestly tell me that there's not a hefty lawsuit in his future?"

Henry smirked. "There might be; Dad was pretty pissed about my baby."

"Your car?" Emma asked in disgust.

"Well, yeah," Henry smacked his lips. "Y'know... if you want me to keep my dad's lawyers out of this, you could be my baby for one night. What do you say?"

Emma gave him an appraising look and smiled sweetly at him. "I'd say..."

"Yeah...?" Henry leaned in close to her as Emma grabbed his right arm and twisted it, pushing his face right onto the nearest metal desk.

"...either you drop it or I'll break your arm into little splinters," Emma said softly. "How does that work for you... baby?"

"FINE! YOU WIN! I'LL LEAVE BOTH OF YOU ALONE!"

"And no lawyers or bribed cops?"

"NOOO! GOOD, GOD — I'LL MAKE SURE OF IT!"

Emma let go of his arm and patted him on the back. "That's a good baby. By the way... your fly's down."

EMMA WAS WALKING TO her locker after class as she spoke on her phone. "Yeah. The medicine is called... oh, man... I don't even know how to pronounce that... it starts with a C, has an R in the middle, and ends in an E. Yeah! That's it! At least, I think so, anyway. It does say that it treats R.A., right? Thank goodness! Okay, I need you to deliver it to 3455 North East Avenue, Regal City Subdivision. Thanks again, Mr. Oswald. Bye."

Emma smiled happily as she got her textbooks out of her locker for English Class. *That's one crisis averted. I can't wait to give Arnold the good news!* She thought excitedly. At times like these, she was happy to be rich and have thirty different pharmacists in her contacts.

She had almost made it to class when she saw Arnold talking to Hector Ramirez. She was about to say "Hi!", when she heard Hector say: "Oh, come on man! First, you go all Viper Kai on Henry Wheeler, which is all over YouTube —"

Arnold shrugged in embarrassment. "Don't remind me. I still don't know who the hell filmed everything that happened. It's just so stupid."

"— and then I see you talking to some hot older chick on your porch this morning that you said you hadn't figured out yet?"

Emma's heart tightened. *Some hot older chick?*

"I told you she's not like that," Arnold waved it off as if it were nothing. "She's just a friend, okay?"

"Hey, no need to defend yourself with me, buddy," Hector grinned. "I'm just happy you're not still pining after Emma. That relationship is never going to happen; it's not worth the time."

"Hey," Arnold shot Hector a small glare. "Emma's worth every second of my time. She's the only girl for me. There's not anyone else who could hold a candle to her."

"That's nice," said Hector as Emma hid behind a row of lockers while the two boys walked by. "It's great to have unrealistic and dangerously high expectations. Maybe, I should make 'High Hopes' your ringtone."

"Just keep it up, Hec," Arnold grinned as he shook his head.

"I'm just saying that you need to keep your options open until you know it's a sure thing."

"Like you and Pria?"

"Exactly, like Pria and me! We're soulmates, y'know? Reincarnated lovers from eons ago in vain of Romeo and Juliet."

"You're a total spaz. You know that, right?"

"Hector Spaz Ramirez. I like the sound of that. Y'know what also has a nice ring to it?"

"What?"

"Mrs. Pria Spaz Ramirez! You think I should run that by her later?"

"Definitely go for it. Put a ring on it."

"But should I do it before or after French Class?"

"See? Now, I can't tell if you're still joking."

"Oh, I am."

"Thank goodness."

"Or am I? I really don't know anymore."

Emma waited until both of their laughter died out and put her head in her hands. *Arnold likes me? Like, really likes me?*

"EMMA? WHAT WERE YOU thinking?" Allison said in exasperation out on the school's football field. Dressed in her cute sports ensemble, Allison prepared for cheerleading tryouts and stretched her legs as she berated her twin.

"Look, I wasn't really going to break his arm," Emma sighed. "...Well, I might have thought about it for a second."

"You can't keep taking risks like that," said Allison, shaking her head in frustration. "Not just because you have a crush on Arnold Regan!"

"I — I don't have a crush on Arnold," Emma said in shock. "I... I don't know how I feel about him."

"Oh, please," Allison scoffed. "You broke Helena's nose for berating him."

"She deserved it!"

"Then you nearly broke Henry's arm for destroying Mrs. Regan's medication."

"I was repaying him for standing up for me!"

Allison rolled her eyes and said, "Since when do you need anyone to stand up for you?"

"Well... I... don't roll your eyes at me! That's my thing!"

"And I saw the charge at Mr. Oswald's Pharmacy in SoHo on our Visa account," Allison smirked. "Care to explain that?"

"I... I... Oh, crap," Emma sighed in comprehension. "I'm crushing on Arnold Regan." Emma let the thought sink in a little more and smiled. "I have a thing for Arnold Regan. And I think he has one for me too."

"Well, duh," Allison laughed. "It's all pretty obvious."

"But how do I... how do I tell him...?"

"That's not for me to decide," said Allison. "I don't even think you and Arnold are good for each other. But I know, you'll have to find that one out for yourself, though."

"Oh, come on, Allison!" Emma pleaded. "You're so much better at this crap than me! This is the one time I actually want you to lecture me."

"I'll try not to take offense to that," Allison sighed. "If you want to, take my Mustang. I can get a ride home with Hiro today, if I need to. All you have to do is pick Ellie up from middle school, and then you can go riding in search of noodle-arms."

"Seriously?"

"You have your license," Allison shrugged. "You might as well use it."

"Did I ever tell you that you're a decent sister?" Emma grinned.

"I could stand to hear it more often," Allison grinned back. "Just promise me you'll stay out of trouble."

"Of course! No worries," Emma smiled as she took in a run.

"There goes Ms. Try-Emma-Everyone-Has!" Emma could hear Helena shouting at her. But that didn't matter; nothing could ruin this feeling... this excitement in her heart.

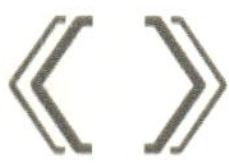

EMMA LOVED HEARING the engine of Allison's Mustang roar as she drove through the city. Though she was eager to drop Ellie off back home. She was ready to talk to Arnold... even if she wasn't sure what to say. But Ellie had convinced her to go get a snack at CK. They had just entered the fast-food hangout as Emma spotted Arnold... sitting across from a striking, older (18 maybe?), girl dressed in a tank top and leather jacket combo with long, black hair, almost down to her waist. This must have been the hot, older chick that Hector mentioned earlier. And she was hot; even Emma had to admit it.

She could just make out what they were talking about.

"I don't know about this, Amelia," Arnold sighed. "I don't think I'm the person you're looking for."

"But don't you owe it to yourself to find out," said Amelia, gazing deeply into his eyes.

"If it's destiny, shouldn't it work itself out anyway?" Arnold said thoughtfully.

"Destiny is a funny thing," said Amelia. "It always struggles against those who fight against it. I know you feel it, don't lie to yourself. Something's changed inside you."

"...You're right," said Arnold. "I can't lie to myself anymore. I guess... I guess I need to give destiny a try for once. I need to give you a try..."

"Emma... what's wrong?" Ellie asked her.

"Nothing's wrong, sis. Did you get your Chicken Fries?"

"Yeah."

"Then, let's go home," said Emma. "I'm getting tired."

"Your meds?"

"Yeah, they're kicking my ass right now," Emma lied, trying not to let there be a catch in her throat. "Let's just go."

WHEN EMMA AND ELLIE got home, Allison and their dad were already setting the table for dinner.

"Hey, girls!" Mr. Berggrias beamed at them.

"Hey, Dad," Emma managed to get out.

"Dad!" Ellie squealed. "I missed you! Why were you gone so long?"

"I had a title to protect, sweetie," Mr. Berggrias smiled as he hugged Ellie and then Emma. "But that's all about to change because... I'm retiring from pro fighting!"

"Really?" Ellie smiled.

"What?" Emma asked in disbelief.

"I know," said Allison. "It's great, isn't it?"

"No, it's not," said Emma. "It's bull-shit! Why would you give up your career, Dad?"

"Well, someone needs to watch over you girls, don't they?" Mr. Berggrias tried his best to force a smile. That might have fooled most people in the world, but not Emma. She knew her dad better than he knew himself.

"Why can't Mom just watch over us like she's been doing?"

The smile on Mr. Berggrias's face faded instantly. "Your mother... why don't we have dinner first and then..."

"...She's gone," said Emma, "isn't she?"

"She's run off with Finn Williams, my old manager," Mr. Berggrias sighed, rubbing his temples.

"Took you long enough to figure that one out," Emma glared.

"Emma — don't!" Allison tried to defuse the situation. "Why don't we all just sit down and talk about this over dinner?"

"It's okay," said Mr. Berggrias. "Truth is, Emma's right, but it doesn't change matters, anyway. I don't know where they've run off to, but they've drained half of fifty bank accounts. We still have enough to live off, to keep all of you girls in school and send each of you to college, but it won't be like it used to. I'm sorry."

"Then you definitely shouldn't retire!" Emma glared at her father, balling her fists. "We can take care of ourselves! Don't give up just because you screwed your marriage over!"

"On the contrary, Emma," Mr. Berggrias said, his eyes flaring, "I think it's obvious you girls need all my attention! Especially you, Emma! Do you know how many blogs, tabloids, and gossip magazines are running articles about your mental illness and sex life? That you've already slept your way through your entire high school after being there for only two days!"

"...You really think that, Dad?"

"...Emma, honey, I'm sorry... I didn't mean to —!"

"No, go ahead," Emma tried to hold back her tears. "Keep on slut-shaming me for something I didn't even do. Call me crazy because I fight to protect my friends. You know why? It just doesn't matter to me. You and your shitty opinion doesn't matter to me anymore. I'm just going to go to my room because I've lost my appetite."

EMMA SLAMMED HER BEDROOM door behind her as tears started pouring down her face. She pounded on her dresser, where she saw pictures of her whole family over the years... as well as her, Hector, and Arnold. She couldn't take it anymore and started shrieking as she cried, throwing the pictures into the wall one by one. The door slowly opened as Allison walked in cautiously.

"Emma, it's going to be okay."

"NO — IT'S NOT! GET OUT!"

"I'm not leaving you, Emma."

"GET OUT! YOU KNEW! YOU KNEW ALL ALONG!"

Emma collapsed on the floor, still sobbing. Allison bent down and hugged her gently. "...No... I didn't."

Chapter Four
Emma
The Fighter

"Emma, someone's here to see you!"

Emma was halfway down the stairs from her bedroom when she heard Ellie calling for her.

"Who is it?" Emma asked dryly.

"It's Arnie," Ellie beamed. "He said that he's here to say thank you for getting his mom her meds... again."

"Tell him to piss off," Emma glared.

"I doubt that's the response he's hoping for," said Ellie sheepishly.

"Well, I really don't care now," said Emma, "do I?"

"Now, Emma, that's not really a way to treat someone," said Mr. Berggrias, who had just entered from the kitchen, still stirring a pot of grits.

"And I definitely don't give a shit about what you think either," said Emma, stubbornly. "ALLISON! ARE YOU READY YET?"

"Geez, Emma," said Allison as she waltzed gracefully down the stairs, not a hair out of place. "You know, Saturday mornings are the times that I record my podcast. ...And I just got done." She added hastily, seeing the expression on Emma's face. "So, I'm ready to go now."

"Good," Emma said in a huff. "Let's go out the garage door."

"Don't you girls want breakfast?" Mr. Berggrias asked.

"No, thanks," Emma replied coolly.

"Well, I might, could go for some —" Allison's voice died out as Emma grabbed her arm and pulled her into the garage.

"What in the hell was that about?" Emma asked her. "I thought you were on my side!"

"Emma, I am," Allison sighed, "but you and Dad just can't keep making the house your own war zone. It's not healthy for anyone."

"I know it's not good for Ellie, okay? I just can't believe Dad would even think those things about me, let alone say them like he did," Emma sighed.

"Well, actually, I meant it wasn't healthy for me and Ellie," Allison replied, massaging her arm. "You have a vice grip for a hand. I swear."

"I'm just not ready to forgive him yet," Emma said firmly. "And I could use your support in this. Because... y'know, we are twins." She gave Allison a begrudgingly pleading look.

"Okay, I'll support you," Allison sighed. "Just don't play the twin card again. You can only use that once every decade. Got it?"

"Got it," Emma grinned.

Allison and Emma each got in the Mustang as the engine started. Allison opened the garage door and started pulling out. "Oh, God! He's still here!"

"Who?" Allison asked, but she smiled weakly at the sight of Arnold trying to flag them down. "Oh, him. Maybe you should try just talking to him. It's been almost a month."

"Just keep driving," Emma hissed.

"Hey! Emma — wait up!"

Allison looked at her sister with concern. "This isn't right."

"Just keep driving," Emma groaned as she sunk deeper into her seat. She could have sworn she heard a defeated Arnold say — "I just want to know what I did wrong..."— *But he knows. He just doesn't want to admit it,* Emma thought quietly as she tried to push Arnold Regan out of her mind.

EMMA FINALLY MADE IT to the school gym. Where her favorite leather punching bag awaited her, with Allison following her inside. "We need to talk about this, Emma."

"Nothing to talk about," said Emma, wrapping masking tape around her knuckles.

"I know things have been difficult lately," said Allison. "For you, more so than any of us. But you have to let someone in."

"I think that you're in close enough," Emma glared.

"I meant Arnold," Allison sighed. "You never even gave him a chance to explain what happened that day you saw him."

"It looked pretty self-explanatory," Emma snarled.

"But hear me out now. Maybe it wasn't," Allison said carefully. "This falling out between the three of you. Arnold doesn't go near Hector anymore. You ignore the hell out of both of them. Hector just spends all of his time with Pria, bossing him around. You were all so close and happy once, and now... you're all alone and miserable. You don't even work out anymore. All you do is just come in here during your free periods and the weekends to punch this stupid bag."

"I thought you didn't think Arnold, and I were good for each other," Emma sighed.

"...I was wrong," said Allison. "It looks like you, Arnold... and even Hector need each other. Just think about it, okay?"

"Whatever," Emma sighed as she started punching the bag.

Allison shook her head and left Emma alone. Emma closed her eyes, picturing the faces of her dad, mom, Helena, and almost everyone else at school, punching and kicking away.

"Nice technique, but your form's off by a long shot," said a grave voice behind her. Emma turned around to see Coach Chris standing behind her. He was wearing red sweats and tennis shoes, his long curly hair giving him the illusion of being a citizen from over a hundred years ago.

"Don't remember asking for your opinion," Emma sighed. "...Anything that I can do for you, Coach?"

"Yeah," he smiled. "The Kickboxing team is having tryouts on Monday. We could use someone with a fire like yours. If you're interested."

"I'm not really a team player," Emma replied.

"Oh, really," Coach chuckled. "How's that working out for you? Tryouts are at three-thirty. Hopefully, I'll see you there."

Coach walked away in a strut that didn't suit him as Emma sat down on the nearest bleacher. She took out her phone and scrolled through years-old photos of her, Arnold, and Hec. They used to be so close; it felt like they could almost read each other's thoughts. The best moments of her life had been with those two bozos. No one in school knew why Arnold and Hec had quit hanging out, but it happened around the time she started ignoring both of them, which had caused rumors to spread like wildfire. She wished things could go back to how they used to be. Like in one pic where they had gone to the fair and rode the Tilt-a-Whirl two-hundred times in a row. Emma almost laughed despite herself when she landed on another of them sneaking into Old Man Garrick's house. Arnold and her had tried to prove to Hec it wasn't haunted. And she still wasn't sure if they'd succeeded.

How can things change so freaking fast? Emma thought as she leaned against the wall of the gymnasium. She sank to the floor, running her fingers through her sweat covered hair. She scrolled passed several other photos, almost every one of them showcasing the trio's beaming faces. Her absolute favorite, though, was the selfie of her and Arnold singing karaoke to the tune of *"Drops Of Jupiter"*. They had grown up together, and now... they were just growing apart.

"EMMA?"

"Hey, Arnold. We need to talk."

Emma had snuck into Arnold's backyard and was sitting on a stack of secondhand brick.

"Funny," he let out a mirthless chuckle, "because I've been trying to talk to you for a month now. But you never seem to have time."

"I've been avoiding you."

"Really? Because I couldn't actually tell. Thanks for pointing that out," Arnold sighed, taking a seat on another stack next to her.

"I see you've kept busy," said Emma, looking at the brick patio Arnold had been building.

"Yeah, but learning how to properly lay brick from YouTube tutorials is a bitch, though," said Arnold. "You learn by trial and error. So, it's a lot of work."

"I see you traded in the old lawnmower, too," Emma observed.

"Yeah," Arnold nodded. "The old riding one gave out, so I traded it in and got a push mower."

"Well, it definitely helped out your physique," said Emma. "You've gone from noodle arms to body builder. I think I've even heard one girl calling you 'Hot Arnold' in the cafeteria last week. You look good."

"It doesn't matter," Arnold said. "I'm not looking for just any girl."

"Because you already have a girlfriend, right?" Emma had seen Arnold after school a few times with that same older-looking girl. They sometimes seemed inseparable.

"What? No!" Arnold exclaimed in shock. "I haven't even been on a single date in my life. Why would you... Oh... Oh! Did you see me with Amelia? Is that what all of this crap has been about?"

"I saw you with her a month ago, saying she was your destiny or something," Emma shrugged.

"I said that because she's a part of my family," Arnold sighed. "We're related, me and her, not a couple."

"But you're with her almost every day," Emma protested.

"Because she's teaching me about my family history," said Arnold. "History my mom doesn't even know about. And she's preparing me..."

"For what?"

"...Do you believe in fate?"

"What?"

"Do you believe everything we are and everything we do is predestined?" Arnold asked as he stared up at the sky.

"Uh, no," said Emma, biting her lip. "Does this have to do with your mom? She's not getting worse, is she?"

"She's not exactly getting better." Arnold shuddered. "Not that you've cared to ask me about her in the past month. But, no, I didn't mean just her. I meant all of us in a way. Because, lately, I feel like I don't have any say in my life or where it's going."

"Like reaching a crossroads at twilight," Emma sighed. Arnold gave her a puzzled look. "It's a phrase I learned in Greece last summer. It's supposed to be a metaphor for either letting the world pick the path it chose for you or you making your own way at a difficult time in your life. One decision. Two possible outcomes."

"What would you do if it were you at the crossroads?"

"That depends on what each one offered," Emma mused. "You got any ideas?"

"One road is the path that everyone else tells you that you'll do great on, but you lose everyone in your life that matters; and the other is you spending your life the way you always wanted to... like riding on a Tilt-a-Whirl with the greatest friends you could ask for, no matter how much it made you want to hurl."

"You did come close to chucking out your guts, didn't you?" Emma grinned.

"Me?" Arnold smiled back. "I was talking about you."

"Okay, so it's all about me now, huh?"

"Oh, definitely," Arnold chuckled, "it always will be."

"Well, after the month I've had," said Emma without hesitation, "I'd never give up my friends again. Because after my mom left us, you were the only one that I wanted to talk to about it."

"I'm sorry, we didn't have the chance," Arnold sighed.

"We have right now," said Emma. "How long of a break can you take?"

"As long as right now is," said Arnold, "which, in my opinion, is however long you want to make it last."

MONDAY WAS THE FIRST cool day of the school year. Emma and Allison gave Arnold a ride that morning. Emma was so happy just to have one of her friends back, she didn't even care that Allison kept smirking at them the entire time. It just felt good to have someone to talk to who wasn't one of her siblings again. Someone who always got her more than most people. Emma even started working out again, for the first time in a month.

And as she and Arnold entered the school together, she told him about Coach's offer.

"You do know that Helena's going to be trying out today too?" Arnold asked, his eyebrow raised.

"That'll just make it more fun," Emma chuckled. "I can take her on my worst day."

"Maybe you should practice before you try out," said Arnold. "It's been a while since you've been in a fight."

"Since when do you know about training?" Emma smiled, clearly bemused.

"Well, I mean, I didn't become 'Hot Arnold' just by mowing lawns."

"Alright, we'll try it right after study hall," said Emma. "That should give us enough time."

"Sounds good," Arnold smiled. "See you then."

Emma smiled as she watched Arnold walk to class.

"I see that you two are... what are you exactly?"

Emma turned around to see Hector standing behind her, wearing a long, black sweater, slacks, and brown dress shoes. The look didn't suit his usual snarky attitude. He also looked a lot paler and skinnier as well.

"I'm not sure," said Emma.

"Yeah, I've been there," said Hector. "In fact, I'm still here. I'm thinking of renaming it Hector's Island. Because Arnold and I haven't really talked in about a month... neither have you and me, come to think of it."

"I didn't mean to — I — it wasn't your fault," Emma stuttered. "I thought Arnold was dating some older girl, and I felt it would be better not to be around either of you since you're both usually a package deal. But it was just a misunderstanding; I'm sorry."

"You don't need to apologize," Hector shrugged. "I never knew you felt that way about him."

"What way?"

"Doesn't matter," said Hector. "Arnold, and I got into a disagreement about Pria."

"Your girlfriend?"

"Yeah," said Hector. "I told him I wanted to go to this student conference with her in a few weeks. He told me I was moving too fast with her and that I was letting her take over my life. We both said some choice words and haven't spoken since."

"I'm certain if you'd just talk to him about what happened, you two could —!"

"I'm willing to listen to what he has to say," Hector sighed, "if he'll actually say it."

Ding! Ding!

Hector checked his phone.

"Shit," Hector muttered. "Pria needs me to carry her books to her locker. It's after chemistry class, so that means it's the thick books! I'll talk to you later, Emma. Let — let Arnold know what I said... if you think it'll matter. See you!"

Emma shook her head. She could see Arnold's point on the subject. She felt her phone vibrate in her backpack and took it out. She had gotten an email from...

"Mom..."

"ARE YOU OKAY?"

Emma was crying in the school gym as she practiced kicks at a punching bag.

"Oh, I'm doing wonderful," she snapped. "Perfect even!"

Arnold gave her a concerned look. "It's your mom, isn't it?"

"What gave it away?" Emma kicked the punching bag so hard it snapped from its chains, flying into the empty bleachers.

"What happened?" Arnold walked over and tried to place his hand on Emma's shoulder.

"NOTHING!" Emma shouted as she went to throw a punch at Arnold's face, which he caught with his hand just in time. He didn't squeeze it, grip it tightly, or try to do any harm. Arnold just lowered her hand gently and gave her a hug as Emma sobbed on his shoulder.

"What did she do?" Arnold asked, his voice calm, caring, and soothing.

"She emailed me," Emma sobbed. "Basically telling me that she doesn't give a shit about any of us, and she'll see me when she sees me, if she sees me."

"Would it make you feel better if I called her a heartless bitch?" Arnold asked. "Because that's what she is, y'know?"

"I don't know," Emma sighed. "Try it?"

"She's a heartless bitch, and you're better off without someone like that in your life," said Arnold. "It's hard to accept at first. You'll blame yourself for some stupid reason or another for a very long time. Then, things will slowly start to get better, and you know life moves on... and even though things are harder in some ways, they're better in the majority of others. That's because the person who caused all of your pain is gone from your life. I know because it happened to me when my dad ran out on my mom and me."

"I don't know if I'm that strong to keep feeling this way any longer," Emma sobbed.

"Yes, you are," said Arnold. "Look at me; you are the strongest person I have ever met. Whether it's in physical or emotional strength. You never give up and you always keep fighting. Because you're a fighter, Emma. You always have been, and just when people are ready to count you out, you prove them wrong. You know why? Your love for everyone you hold dear in your life fuels you. Nothing can stop a force that fights for those she loves. You're unstoppable."

Emma gave Arnold a watery smile. "You sure know how to give a pep talk."

"I mean, I have been practicing."

"Have you?"

"Every day in the mirror, before I get dressed in the morning. You should see me; I'm always a mess. But it helps to get a good cry in —"

Emma leaned in and gave Arnold a passionate kiss. His eyes widened as he returned it with his own. When they stopped, each grinned, as Arnold said, "Not that I'm complaining... but what was that for?"

"You were rambling," Emma chuckled, "and I didn't want it to ruin your great pep talk."

"Does this mean... what I want it to mean?" Arnold asked, sheepishly.

"That you can be a rambling idiot sometimes?"

"Oh, I..."

"...And that you're also sensitive, kind, and I care about you," said Emma. "That if you asked me on a date, I would seriously consider it."

"How about after tryouts?"

"Only if I make the team."

"I'll take that as a yes."

AS IT SO HAPPENS, EMMA made the team. Though Helena gave her a hell of a fight this time around. Apparently, she had been training with Hector's older brother, her boyfriend, Xander, ever since Emma broke her nose. The fight lasted for almost forty-five minutes, as neither one wanted to give in. But Emma, remembering Arnold's pep talk, focused on all the love she had in her life as she felt a surge of energy flow through her body. Emma then won the fight with a swift tornado kick.

Currently, Emma and Arnold were leaving Galaxy Coffee. Their date had gone amazingly well. They talked about almost everything. Occasionally, Arnold would get nervous and Emma would reach out, grip his hand, as they would both just smile at each other. They were walking down Main Street, still sipping on their coffees, as a man bumped into Arnold.

"Son of a..."

"Arnold...?"

Emma's date fell to his knees. Emma almost screamed when she saw that Arnold's stomach was bleeding like mad from a freshly made stab wound... but his blood was golden?

"Arnold!"

Emma took out her phone and tried to call 911, but the man who had stabbed Arnold jumped her. Emma fell on her back inside a nearby alley. Her attacker wore a long coat, sunglasses, and fedora, carrying a large black dagger.

"GET THE HELL — AWAY FROM ME!"

Emma gave a swift spin kick, knocking the attacker on his back. Emma got to her feet as the attacker shot up into the air... with its wings flapping violently?

"What the hell are you?" Emma muttered.

The attacker's hat and glasses had fallen off, revealing a scarred, wrinkled, bald face with cat eyes, large fangs, and long claws for hands. If Emma didn't know better, she would have sworn that it was a...

"Harpy?"

The creature swarmed down at her as Emma saw flashes of the same visions that had been haunting her nightmares — herself fighting in a war against gods and monsters from Greek mythology. Just like it had really been Emma who fought those battles — and she was a goddess — she leaped to the fire escape — then, on instinct, tried to unsheathe two daggers. She gasped when she felt two silver daggers actually appear in her hands. "...No freaking way..." Emma muttered to herself as she leaped at the Harpy, stabbing its chest with her blades. The Harpy let out a loud shriek as it stabbed Emma in her arm, forcing the girl to fall to the ground.

"Damn't!" Emma cursed as she saw her daggers land a few feet away from her. The Harpy, still holding its weapon, was flying right at her... until it wasn't. The Harpy crashed into the nearest dumpster with an axe poking out of its back. And Arnold walking quickly behind it. His stab wound almost completely healed. Arnold grabbed the Harpy's head with one hand and the axe's hilt with the other. He made two quick pulls in the opposite directions, and the Harpy exploded into ash.

"How in the hell — did you do that?" Emma gasped. Good lord, did her arm hurt.

"I'm the God of War," said Arnold as he helped her up.

"No, really," Emma winced.

"It's the truth," Arnold said, somberly. "And you're the Goddess of Love. That's why the Harpy, one of the Four Horsemen, attacked us."

"You can't be serious," said Emma in disbelief.

"When you were in Greece," said Arnold, "did you learn what ichor was?"

"Yeah."

"Good," Arnold grinned, despite himself. "Look at the blood coming from your arm."

Emma looked at her injured arm and nearly had a heart attack. She was bleeding golden blood... she was bleeding ichor.

"We need to get to the Hoof," said Arnold. "So, the kids can check you out and fill you in on everything."

"Whose kids?"

"...Ours."

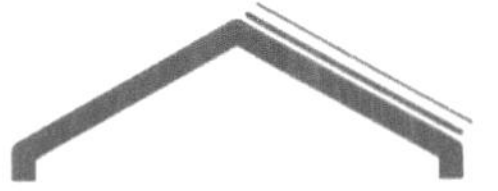

Chapter Five
Arnold
The Four Horsemen

"You're joking, right?"

"Emma... if you'll just hear them out," Arnold sighed.

"We're not gods, Arnold!"

"As hard as it is to believe, Mother —" Tristan started.

"DON'T CALL ME THAT!" Emma shouted furiously.

Arnold had brought her to the Hoof, an abandoned warehouse outside the city limits that Tristan and Amelia had turned into a personal Olympian training facility. It was where Arnold spent the past month learning how to master his growing godly abilities, and where he received his Deicide axe.

"Emma, I can prove it," said Arnold. "If you'll let me."

"I KNOW WHO I AM!"

"Then how would you explain the Harpy attacking us in the alley tonight?"

"...Arnold," Emma grabbed his shoulder and pulled him over to the side. "I can't be someone else. Especially not a goddess and a mother. I'm barely able to handle going to school and living with my dad. How in the hell could I deal with... all of this shit. I'll really lose my mind if..."

"I don't like this either, Emma," said Arnold. "But we're and everyone we love is in danger. That Harpy was one of the Four Horsemen of the Apocalypse. They are harbingers of Twilight. They won't stop until they kill us because we're the only ones who can put an end to it."

"You're not making any sense," said Emma as a tear rolled down her face.

"I will, if you just let me show you what I'm talking about," Arnold pleaded. "We can't run from who we are."

"I... can't," said Emma, "I can't do this!"

Emma then took off at a run, leaving Arnold and their children behind.

"She was always stubborn," Tristan sighed. "Give her time, Father. She'll come around soon enough. Until then, I'll keep a watch over her."

"That's okay, Tristan," said Arnold. "If she sees you, she'll freak."

"But the Horsemen..."

"Won't lay a finger on her," said Arnold calmly, "because I'll be there to protect her."

"But what about your..." Amelia started.

"I can split my duties up a little more," said Arnold, "after all, who needs sleep?"

FOR THE NEXT THREE days, Arnold spent his time in four ways: Going to school, training at the Hoof, taking care of his mother, and watching Emma from the trees outside her bedroom window. Each night, Arnold wished he could lie beside her, holding her gently in his arms. As he slowly drifted into a reluctant sleep, Arnold remembered how his journey to this point began...

"YOU ARE THE GOD OF War, Father," said Amelia. "You were the leader of Zeus's armies!"

"Then what happened?"

"Zeus and his brothers, Poseidon and Hades, led a revolt against the true King of Gods. They failed miserably, just as Lucifer did before them."

"Wait a minute... you're not saying..."

"Yes," said Amelia. "The Olympians were originally God's highest-ranking angels, until they broke his most sacred law. They conceived children with mortals. These children were deemed too dangerous and destructive because of the angelic blood mixing with a mortal's would usually result in the creation of a demon, so, after countless of these children caused a terrifying massacre, God sent his most trusted warrior, Uriel, down to slay them all when they were of age. Barely any of them survived."

"Oh, god..."

"Zeus was outraged, so he gathered the Olympians together to try and overthrow God... and when that failed, a traitor amongst the Olympians was given the task of punishing the others. He cast a curse that would scatter his brothers and sisters somewhere in time but stripped of their identities and powers. Then, on the year of Twi-

light, the Four Horsemen would track them down and kill every last one of them. Only Hades managed to escape."

"It's hopeless, then," sighed Arnold. "There's no fighting God's will."

"But that's not the end of the story," said Amelia. "God decreed that night, a few Olympians could retain a portion of their powers, and if they could use it to slay the Four Horsemen — all the remaining Olympians would be allowed to live and Mount Olympus would be reborn. Where the revived Olympians could serve as protectors of the world, as they always should have been. All you have to do is let us train you for this fight. Please... Father... please."

"HEY, DUMBASS!"

Arnold jolted awake as he fell out of the tree. "Damn't!" He cursed under his breath. Arnold stood up in a tired daze, rubbing his eyes. Emma was standing in front of him, rolling hers.

"You can't keep doing this," she glared.

"Oh, I don't know," Arnold sighed. "I've been falling on my ass since I was six, and it hasn't caused any real damage."

"You can't keep spying on me," Emma snarled. "I told you that I didn't want anything to do with that life."

"Well, I guess I can just stop and go home then... oh... wait... You're still an Olympian who is being hunted by the Four Horsemen. Whether you accept your real identity or not, your life is in danger. And I refuse to let the one woman I love die! So, I guess I can keep doing this!" Arnold snapped irritably.

Emma looked at him in shock; her eyes widened. "Did you just say that you... that you're... in love with me?"

"What gave it away?" Arnold sighed. "...You honestly couldn't tell how I feel about you? After all these years. It's been you. It's always been you."

Emma looked like she wanted to scream as she punched her fist into the wall of her house.

"Emma! Are you —?" Arnold started.

"Oh, god, do you have any idea what you're doing to me?" Emma snarled as she stormed off in anger.

Arnold leaned up against the tree trunk and took a deep breath. "...Sometimes I think she should be the God of War."

THE DAY ONLY GOT WORSE as school started. Arnold failed three tests, which resulted in him receiving afternoon detention. When he arrived in the mostly deserted classroom, seeing Emma and Hector there surprised Arnold. Principal Gia was the one who would be residing over their shared three hours of misery.

"Mr. Regan, so nice of you to join us," said Principal Gia. "Please, take your seat."

Arnold nodded and took one in the middle of Emma and Hector. Hector raised his hand.

"Yes, Mr. Ramirez?"

"I really think this is unfair, m'am," said Hector. "What I did might have been a little unethical, but it didn't really hurt anyone."

"You cheated in the class elections," Principal Gia sneered. "You should be expelled for stuffing the ballot box. So, be thankful I'm allowing you to stay in school."

"Yes, m'am."

Emma raised her hand.

"Yes, Ms. Berggrias?"

"Can I serve my detention on another afternoon?" Emma asked desperately.

"What's wrong?" Principal Gia sneered. "Not comfortable around your old lover?"

Emma squeezed her fist tightly as she tried to control her temper. "I haven't screwed anyone, especially not Arnold."

"Perhaps you have, and you just can't remember," Principal Gia smirked. "I mean, that's the thing about the wrath of heaven, isn't it? The lord just has a wonderful sense of irony. Turning the slutty Goddess of Love, who only cared about peace and prosperity, into a bitter, bitchy young girl who fears her own emotions. And her lover, the God of War, into a weak pacifist. I just had to take a moment to savor this."

"...You're one of them," said Arnold. "You're one of the Four Horsemen!"

"Oh, god," said Emma, "not another bird-bitch."

Hector looked at Emma and Arnold, confused. "What are you three talking about?"

"Hector," said Arnold, "run! Now!"

"But where is he going to run, Ares?" Principal Gia laughed as she raised her hands, and the ground beneath them started to convulse. The classroom floor burst open as roots from the trees outside and vines wrapped around their bodies.

"WHAT THE HELL IS THIS?" Hector shouted.

"HOW IS SHE DOING THIS?" Emma screeched.

"SHE'S FREAKING MOTHER NATURE — THAT'S HOW! SHE'S THE EARTH GODDES GAI!"

"Guilty," Gai laughed. "I would say this isn't personal, but I always did hate Aphrodite. So arrogant. And for what? It sure wasn't your IQ or battle skills that drove men and gods wild. But, at least now, you leveled out some, sweetie. Too bad, it's a millennium too late."

Gai walked over and stroked Emma's face gently.

"DON'T TOUCH ME!"

Emma tore free of the vines restraining her and tackled Gai. Arnold heard a loud slash as ichor splattered around the classroom. The roots around Arnold and Hector vanished as Emma stood up over Gai's dead body, two silver daggers gleaming in her hands. When she turned to look at Arnold, it was like staring into the eyes of a raging animal. "Two down, two to go."

"Oh, so now you believe me," Arnold said with a small smile.

"Well, when the ground opens up and tries to drag you to hell, it's pretty hard not to," said Emma. "I'll help you kill the other two horsemen, but I'm not her anymore. I don't want to be, and I'm not going back. No matter who claims to be our kids."

Before Arnold could protest —

"What in the hell are you two talking about?" Hector interrupted nervously. "You two aren't — you can't be —!"

"It's a long story, Hec," Arnold sighed, shaking his head.

"And where did those freaking daggers come from?"

"Those are her Deicides," said Arnold. "Every Olympian is bound to one. Deicides are weapons made in the forges of heaven that can kill any angel who claimed to be a god. It's one of the few things that's deadly to all of us. We can only summon them in times of great danger."

"All I did was get pissed off," Emma shrugged.

"We don't always do it willingly," said Arnold. "Most of the time, it's by instinct. Watch."

Arnold raised his arm and acted like he was going to throw a football as his large silver axe materialized, flying into the chalkboard in front of them. The axe then flew back into Arnold's waiting hand.

"Okay, that was cool," said Hector. "But all of this shit can't be real, right? It's crazy!"

"Welcome to my world," Emma let out a mirthless laugh.

"We had better get out of here," said Arnold. "If one of the Horsemen had been hidden inside the school this whole time —"

"— then it isn't safe," Emma finished.

The trio walked out of the classroom and into the deserted hallway as someone came running towards them.

"Pria?" Hector asked in shock.

His girlfriend wrapped her arms around him as Arnold rolled his eyes, and Emma raised her eyebrow.

"I felt the earthquake and knew you were still here," said Pria. "So, I came to make sure you were still okay!"

"Yeah, honey, I'm fine," said Hector. "Thanks to Arnold and Emma, anyway."

"I'm so... happy to hear that," said Pria as she kissed Hector.

Emma nudged Arnold on his shoulder.

"What?"

"Something's wrong," she whispered.

"Tell me about it."

"No, dumbass," Emma looked in a panic. "Pria doesn't love him! I — I can feel it somehow! She doesn't love anyone. Her soul is — empty!"

"How do you —?"

"I don't know," said Emma, "but trust me — Pria's not human!"

BANG!

"HECTOR!"

Arnold and Emma's screams came too late as Hector fell to the floor, bleeding in his chest. Pria stood above him, smirking as she held the still-smoking pistol.

"WHAT DID YOU DO?" Emma shouted at her.

"Just wait for it," Pria sneered.

"Oh, good lord," Arnold gasped. "Amelia was right."

The bullet in Hector's stomach popped out in a second as his gunshot wound healed instantly. He looked up at Pria in shock and horror. "What just happened? Why? How did you —?"

"I had to be certain," Pria sneered. "You're not a god like your friends here. But you are a demigod... Son of Hades."

Chapter Six
Arnold
Hell Have No Fury...

"Have you freakin' lost your mind!" Hector snarled. "I have a father, and he's not a god!"

"Oh, him?" Pria smirked. "You were adopted, sweetie. Didn't anyone ever tell you? The ruler of the underworld's ichor runs through your veins. And soon... he will come to claim you."

"Why wait until now?" Arnold asked. "Hades created Hector ages ago. Why would he come now?"

"Because the Twilight of the Gods is approaching, Ares," Pria giggled. "It's not just a thing where you all get reunited and get redemption. When all of us awaken, the final stages of this pitiful mortal world will begin. Either angels or the Olympians will reign over the mortals and decide their fate. It is a war to decide whether the real God will save the world or the Olympians will damn it. But I guess your bitch of a daughter left those details out. Imagine that."

"You're one of... us?" Emma asked.

"I was once," Pria glared at the thought. "My name was Persephone. I was Hades's wife. Until I saw what he... and all of you were capable of. The innocent people you slaughtered. You weren't gods, angels, or demons... you were much worse. Every tragedy that happened over the centuries has been all your fault. This wasn't the first time you all were reborn. This has been happening since before Christ and is still a plague that has yet to be stopped. Do you even remember what hellish atrocities you committed for Olympus?"

"You're lying," Arnold growled.

"You weren't actually under the delusion that you were the heroes of this story, were you?" Pria let out a mirthless laugh. "Just four years ago, Hades unleashed a Beast he created that almost wiped out every reality in existence. The only reason that didn't happen was because a group of Chosen mortals slew it on the ruins of Camelot. And you know why Hades did that? Why did he risk trillions of lives? Because he was preparing for Twilight, for the day he would be reunited with his family! All of you! Who were at times even worse than him! The only difference was, he escaped before he could be punished!"

"...She's telling the truth," said Emma in horror. "I can sense her honesty, her righteousness. That's why she doesn't have a soul; she chose not to have one."

"How is that possible?" Hector asked in shock.

"Having souls was what damned all of you," Pria sighed. "It's what drove all of you to the brink. Angels were never supposed to have souls like the mortals do! We're different from them — we can't — it destroys us! Only a few of our family agreed not to go through with obtaining one, and we were the only ones who remained pure because of it!"

"Who else sided with you?" Arnold asked.

"You'll see soon enough," Pria shrugged. Pria aimed her gun and fired three shots as the world faded to black.

"YOU MUST BE — STRONGER!" Tristan yelled as he whipped Arnold's bareback.

"I'm trying!" Arnold shouted in agony.

"Trying isn't good enough!"

Arnold was inside the Hoof, supporting three car engines above his head as Tristan continued to strike him.

"Do you think the Four Horsemen will go easy on you or Mother?" Tristan snarled. "Because they won't! They will only stop after dragging you to hell!"

"I told you that I —!"

"What? Aren't good enough? That we're wrong about you? Well, we're not! You are Ares, the God of War! And it's time you accept that. Stop being weak, Father! Or do you just want to lie down and beg for your life when the time comes? Because it will! They'll kill your love, your friends... and the woman who raised you. Hell, they'll probably start with her first. What will you do when they're all screaming out your name in terror, begging you to save them? But all you do is... nothing."

"SHUT UP!"

Arnold threw the engines at Tristan, causing him to fall down the nearest stairway. Tristan stood up, shaking it off, and smirked. "Now that... is stronger."

"Why the hell did you just do that to me?" Arnold asked in frustration. "I COULD HAVE KILLED YOU!"

"Hardly," Tristan scoffed. "As for why I did it — you're the God of War; your powers come from anger and fury. When used properly, your rage makes you stronger than any of the others. The hard part is getting you to acknowledge it! And stop being a bloody pussy!"

"...You're right."

ARNOLD WOKE UP, SHACKLED in the basement next to Hector.

"Dear God, I've got a massive headache," Arnold muttered. "What did that bitch do to us?"

"I think she shot us in our damn heads," Hector moaned. "At least your wound has already healed; I still have blood running down my face."

"Where's Emma?" Arnold asked as he tried to break his chains unsuccessfully.

"I don't know," Hector sighed. "I just woke up a few seconds before you did."

"Great," Arnold let out a mirthless laugh. "Just freaking wonderful! I was supposed to protect her... and you."

"Me too, huh?" Hector chuckled. "I'm flattered. Is that why we haven't spoken for a damn month?"

"Amelia, my fully grown immortal daughter, told me she thought you were a demigod," Arnold sighed. "Which were the children sired by mine and Emma's people, and those kids usually turned out to be the worst kind of demons imaginable. They would commit even worse sins than us, apparently. So, they were all killed by the angel Uriel. And if he or anyone else had discovered, you were the last surviving demigod… well, y'know? So, she asked me to keep my distance from you. That way, the Horsemen couldn't gain your scent when they attacked me."

"That's why you started the fight with me about Pria?"

"Yeah."

"You never had a problem with her?"

"I wouldn't say that."

"Good," Hector laughed. "At least one of us has good taste in girls. I just wish you would have been honest about all this shit. I would have listened to you."

"Really?"

"Well, you would've had to do your cool magic trick with a battle-axe, but yeah."

"I'm sorry, man," Arnold sighed. "I screwed up so freaking much. I trained my ass off for a month because I was convinced I was supposed to be this great warrior god who was going to save and redeem his people. But it turns out it wasn't even like that. I was a monster. We all were. If we did any of what Pria suggested… maybe we deserve to go to hell. There might not be any hope of redemption for us."

"Bullshit," said Hector, bluntly. "Did you ever even read your Bible or go to church?"

"Not for years."

"Then think hard about this," Hector said calmly. "God forgives; it's that simple. It doesn't matter what shitty things you do; as long as you feel remorse, he forgives you. Which means if he thinks all of us are worth a damn, then we can all find some kind of redemption. It's just a simple fact. If you want to avoid being the monster you used to be, then just do it! Change your destiny while you can. Be who you want to be, not who everyone tells you to. Because the Arnold and Emma I know, are the best damn friends a guy could ever ask for. I mean, look at me. Apparently, I made out with my biological father's ex-wife, and I'm not going to give up on myself because of it."

"Actually, I'm not sure if they ever divorced."

"Well, damn," Hector frowned and let out a low whistle. "I did screw up on that one, didn't I? Doesn't matter, though. I'll make up for that mistake. We all will,"

"You got a lot of faith in people who don't deserve it," Arnold smiled sadly.

"No, I don't," said Hector. "I have faith in my friends. Always have."

"I hate to interrupt this little reunion," came a familiar voice from up the school stairs.

Arnold recognized it immediately. "You have to be kidding me!"

"I'm afraid not," Amelia smiled as she fully entered the basement.

"You both played me from the beginning," Arnold snarled.

"I did," Amelia laughed. "But Tristan didn't. He actually loves you and Mother."

"And you don't?" Arnold gritted his teeth.

"Not really," Amelia said casually. "You see, I was made by you… with a mortal woman centuries ago. I still remember when I slit her throat and watched her blood drip into her dinner. I thought I would feel bad at first, but I just wondered if you would be proud of me. But you weren't… you beat me within an inch of my life… until Uriel came and finished the job. I lost count of how long I burned in hell. But then Persephone came and offered me a chance to get my vengeance, and I took it."

"What vengeance?" Arnold rolled his eyes. "You killed your own mother? What did you expect me to do?"

"YOU WERE MY FATHER!" Amelia shrieked. "YOU SIRED ME! YOU MADE ME THE DEMON THAT I AM! AND YOU TURNED YOUR BACK ON ME! ON ALL OF US!"

"I'm sensing some deep-rooted issues," said Hector. "I know you've been in hell for a very long time, but we now have these wonderful new experiences called: Family Therapy. And I think you two could really benefit from it. And I already know this great doctor. What do you say?"

Amelia gave an evil smirk and stabbed Arnold in his chest.

"I don't think she's crazy about that idea, Hec," Arnold groaned.

"No, but she is crazy," said Hector.

Amelia leaned in close over Hector. "I think I'll slit your throat first."

"Amelia — that's enough!" Pria said as she entered the base-ment. "Unchain Ares." Pria removed a long, thin black blade from the sheathe she was now wearing around her waist.

"Deicide," Arnold muttered. "You're going to unchain me, then try to kill me? I think you got this whole murder thing backwards. It's easier to kill someone who can't fight back."

"Dude, don't give her pointers," Hector sighed. "Do you want them to kill us?"

"Deicide can only kill an Olympian when used honorably," said Pria, raising her eyebrow at Hector. "As one of the Four Horsemen, I must abide by my lord's rules. Now, Amelia, un-chain your father."

"Yeah... about that..."

Amelia spun around and kicked Pria in her chest as the angel's sword flew into the air. Amelia caught it happily and ran it through Pria's heart. She smirked gleefully. "There's been a change of plans. I may be as pretty as an angel, but I was never even close to being one. So, I'm not bound by your lord's rules, Persephone! Have fun wherever the slain angels go... or don't."

Amelia turned back to face Arnold and Hector. And used the Deicide to stab Arnold four more times and slashed Hector six. Their blood poured on the floor as their wounds had already begun to heal. Amelia then used the Deicide to carve runes into the blood-drenched floor.

"What are you doing?" Arnold growled.

"I wasn't the only child you let down, Father," Amelia smirked. "There's so many of them suffering in hell as we speak. So, I think it's time they get out on parole: good behavior and all that. Your ichor, combined with Hector's demigod blood, will open a portal to hell for all of them to walk through. The only other thing I need is the right tool to channel such power."

"The Deicide!" Arnold gasped. "Amelia — don't do this. There's no guarantee that only your siblings will come out. You could unleash all of hell on earth. Billions of innocent people will die!"

"Look at you being so damn noble," Amelia snickered. "It's pathetic. Since when do you care about anyone besides your idiotic Olympians? You used to slaughter these innocent people, just like I did. Only you punished me for it. You punished all of us. You were a hypocrite then... and a fool now. I couldn't believe how easy it was to gain yours and Tristan's trust. You both are so arrogant and trusting! All it took was stroking your ego. And now, look at both of you. Like father, like son, eh?"

"What did you do to him?" Arnold snarled.

"Oh, don't worry," Amelia laughed. "He's still alive. I've decided the first one you love who will die is going to be your precious Aphrodite…"

"Don't you touch her!"

"…Or perhaps your weak mortal mother," Amelia smirked. "I wonder just how much I could make her beg… while I make you watch."

"Y'know what, Amelia," Arnold snarled as his eyes flashed dark red. "Thanks. You just said the magic words!"

Arnold busted free from his chains, summoning his own Deicide to his hand. "The angrier I get, the more powerful I am, and you just pissed me off!"

Arnold swung his axe at Amelia, who countered with her sword. Arnold struck down harder as she kicked his right leg. Arnold smiled. "Nice try. But that didn't even tickle. Look's like you should have killed Tristan first! Because he taught me how to survive!" Arnold swung the axe cleanly through her left leg, severing it completely from the bone. "Or did he forget to mention that?"

Amelia let out a loud shriek of laughter. "Oh, how I dreamed of this moment! My father, the evil and vicious Ares, reborn! Now, you'll never be able to go back to being that annoyingly sweet boy again. I've made the real you return! And now there's no going back. No redemption… for you…"

Arnold paused at her words, his powerful anger wavering. So Amelia took her chance and threw Persephone's sword into the blood-powered runes as they glowed a hellish crimson. The portal to hell slowly opened. "NO!"

Arnold swung his axe at Amelia one last time as her head fell to the ground with a loud thud. Arnold turned back to Hector and quickly cut him free from his chains. Hector ran over to Arnold, his voice quivering when he spoke. "What are we going to do now?"

"I don't know."

"My, my, this is a dreadful place for a family reunion."

Arnold turned around and saw a tall, thin, black, bald man dressed in a grey suit. His eyes flickering with an insidious shimmer. Behind him stood Emma, holding the severed head of Henry Wheeler by its hair.

"Emma… good, lord… what did you do?"

Emma's eyes widened as if she was seeing Arnold for the first time in a century. She quickly suppressed a shudder, then glanced at Henry's head and tossed it nonchalantly into the portal. "I'm not Emma… not anymore."

"You… remember?" Arnold gasped in shock.

"Everything," Emma sighed. "Including that Henry was Hephaestus… one of two traitors to our family and the final Horseman."

"…How?"

"Him," Emma jerked her head towards the man standing closest to her.

"Who —?"

"Uh, not to ruin this really strange and awkward identity crisis," said Hector, "but there is the small matter of a freaking portal to hell about to unleash your demented kids!"

The man in the suit smiled warmly. "Not to worry, my boy. I can make quick work of this… with your help."

Hector grimaced at the thought. "Me? No, no, no! You have to — are you nuts?"

"You are a child of death," the man grinned. "My child."

"You're…?"

"He's telling the truth," Emma looked as if she was forcing herself to say these words. "Ares, this is one of the three eldest Olympians, those who paved the way to our creation… our family, and he is also your father, Hector. His name is Hades. You can both trust him."

"…That's — it can't be —!" Hector stuttered.

"I can prove it," said Hades as he placed his hand on Hector's shoulder. "I can do for you what I did for Aphrodite. I can give you back your memories, your true identity. You just have to let me."

"I don't know, man," said Hector, the panic obvious in his voice.

"Hector, you don't have to do this if you don't want to," Arnold said plainly. "There could be another way."

"Ares," said Emma, walking over to Arnold in such a graceful fashion, it looked as if she was gliding on air. "Hades is our brother." She caressed Arnold's cheek gently. "He would never hurt his son or any friend of ours. I was hesitant too, remember? But you insisted that I embrace who I am."

"Maybe I was wrong," said Arnold. "I'm not sure who we can trust right now, Emma. Amelia was a sociopath! How do we know that anything she said was real? I've had nightmares of this man, and he kills me in them every night! How can you believe a word he says?"

"You must have faith in him… and me, my love." Emma leaned in and kissed Arnold passionately as a slight glaze overtook his eyes for a moment. "...You're right," Arnold replied as their lips gently parted. "Hec, we can trust Hades."

"Seriously?" Hector glared at them. "We don't even —!"

Emma walked over to Hector and whispered in his ear, "Hades is your true father. Trust him. Let him restore your true self. Let him in."

"...Okay," said Hector as if he was in a daze. He turned his gaze to Hades. "I trust you, Father."

"That's all I needed to hear... Son," Hades smiled as he placed his fingers on Hector's forehead and both their eyes turned dark. Hades's eyes soon returned to normal, as did Hector's; they then shared a smile of disbelief and joy. "Father?"

"Yes, Son," Hades smiled as a tear ran down his face. "It's me."

"I thought I lost you," Hector threw his arms around Hades as tears flooded his face. "It's been far too long!"

"I know," Hades chuckled, "but we'll have time to catch up later. Right now, we have a small bit of trouble to resolve."

Hector nodded as he and Hades walked over to the portal, raising their hands high above it. Black energy shot out of their hands and into the swirling vortex, slowly devouring it entirely. The smoking skull of Henry Wheeler lying in its place.

Arnold blinked in amazement. "How did you guys do that?"

"We have a connection to hell," said Hector, staring at Arnold, "since we draw our powers from death. But it was really Hephaestus's head that got the job done."

Arnold looked over at Emma, who raised her eyebrow, "You didn't think I beheaded him just because he screwed us over, did you?"

"It did cross my mind," Arnold shrugged. "...So, was that it? Is Twilight over?"

Hades chuckled, shaking his head. "No, my dear brother, I'm afraid not. For Twilight to truly be complete, we must defeat the champion our father has selected to represent him."

"That's not the story I heard," Arnold said.

"Amelia didn't tell you the truth?" Hades smirked. "What a surprise! Well, as you said quite accurately earlier, she was a sociopath and had her own agenda. But there were pieces of truth mixed in with her lies. Yes, we had to defeat the Four Horsemen as a small part of Twilight. But that was just to see which of us would be the chosen of our family for the final battle. A match against a human wielding a godly weapon of untold power. If we kill him, Mount Olympus will return to life, and we will replace our father as the true rulers of all the realms."

"No," said Arnold. "I'm not killing some random guy to overthrow God! I don't want any part of this!"

Emma smiled at Arnold with concern and kissed him again. "Don't worry, Ares. Hades has his most trusted men guarding and taking care of your mortal mother. And after we defeat God's champion, we'll have the power to heal her of all her afflictions."

"She's right," said Hector. "My father would never lie. We were the ones who were wronged. We were the victims. And now we have to take back what should have been ours all along."

"I don't…"

Emma kissed Arnold again. "Please, my love. Trust us."

Arnold blinked sleepily before shaking it off. "Fine. Who is it we have to kill?"

Hades smirk widened.

"A young man named Jason Gardner."

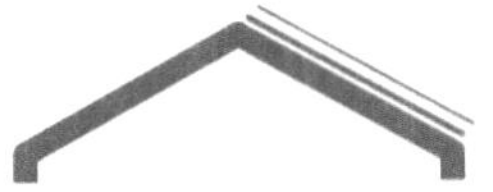

Epilogue
Emma
A Darker Form Of Love

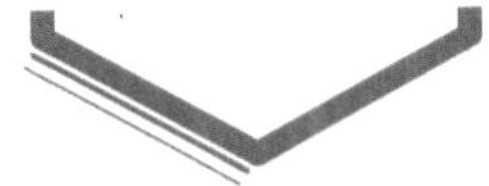

"*Why did you save me?*"

"*Because you're my sister. The same ichor that runs through your veins also courses through mine. But of course, you don't remember that as of yet. But never fear, just as I have slain this pathetic Fourth Horseman, I will restore you to your true identity.*"

The man gestured at the slaughtered body of the monster, who claimed to be Medusa. She had almost turned Emma to stone... almost. Bronze ropes still bound Emma to a chair in the middle of the school gym.

"*Look — I want to avoid remembering whatever the hell 'we' were,*" *Emma snarled.* "*So, just go find someone else to screw around with!*"

"*Oh, I'm afraid this isn't a choice, sister,*" *the man smirked.* "*The true Twilight is fast approaching, and I need my family at their peak.*"

The man grasped Emma's head as she screamed out in agony, a million memories from a different life returning to her instantly.

"EMMA?"

Allison had just flipped the light on in her bedroom to find her sister leaning up against the bedpost. Emma gave her a weak smile.

"Hey, Allison." Emma couldn't help but stare at her. So much had changed in just a few hours. It was hard to believe who her annoyingly superior sister once was and the person she had become.

"Where have you been?" Allison ran over and hugged Emma. "Everyone thinks you died in that earthquake at the school! Dad and Ellie have been worried senseless. We've spent the better part of the night looking for you! We —!"

Emma threw her arms around Allison, returning her embrace tightly.

"...Uh, Emma?" Allison asked in shock. "Remember when I said you had a vice grip?"

Emma let go quickly, looking at Allison in an expression of pure grief. "Sorry, sis."

"What happened to you?" Allison asked, her eyes examining Emma as if searching for proof of a mental meltdown.

"...I'm having to leave home for a while," said Emma, finally. "And will you quit staring at me like that? It's freaking me out!"

"I'm freaking you out?" Allison asked, outraged. "You just told me that you're running away!"

"I'm not running away," Emma assured her. "I just have some unfinished business to take care of. I'll be back home soon, I promise."

"Yeah, just like Mom did?" Allison glared at her. "You're going to look for her, aren't you?"

"No!" Emma said in disgust. "I never want to see that bitch again."

"Then, what in the hell — is so important that you have to abandon our family?"

"...Allison, look me in the eye," said Emma plainly, "and I'll explain everything."

"Fine," Allison huffed.

As soon as they made eye contact, Emma grasped Allison's forehead. Allison's eyes turned golden as she fell to the ground. When she struggled back up, Allison gasped in shock.

"...Aphrodite?"

"Hello, Athena," Emma smiled sadly.

"Twilight has come?"

"Yes, it has," Emma sighed.

"Hades!" Allison snarled. "All this for his son? He and Apollo betrayed us for their damned uprising?"

"I get it; you're pissed," Emma rolled her eyes.

"Look at what I'm wearing!" Allison gestured at her pink leather jacket, turquoise blouse, black mini-skirt, and matching heels.

"I thought that was your favorite outfit?" Emma snickered.

"It is! Or it was?" Allison shook her head, confused, and irritated. "I love being a cheerleader, but I also think it's demeaning! It's like I'm both Athena and Allison! I don't know which one is really me! Why aren't you feeling this way?"

"Because it doesn't matter what was real," Emma said, "all that does is who I want to be."

"And you called me annoying?" Allison glared at her.

"Which you?" Emma smirked. "Allison or Athena?"

"Oh, shut up," Allison sighed, "you're giving me a headache."

"Well, it's about to get worse," Emma said darkly. "Hades found his son. If he wins Twilight, they'll rule the realms, which will be horrible for everyone, including us. And he wants me to help them do it."

"You can't be serious?" Allison asked in disgust. "Why on earth would you help those bastards?"

"...Because of Ares," Emma said after a long pause.

"He's in this city too?"

"Ares is Arnold," Emma said, her brow furrowing in disconcertion. "It figures that even after centuries of our identities being constantly rewritten, I would still fall in love with him every single time. Some sort of divine sense of irony, I guess. Hades threatened to return all of Ares's memories to Arnold if I didn't agree to serve him in Twilight."

"Oh, yeah," Allison let out a mirthless laugh. "Unleash the unstable and unstoppable God of War that even the supposed God of Death couldn't defeat by himself. That's a wonderful idea!"

"Which is why I accepted his offer," Emma sighed. "I used the Charm to entrance both Arnold and Hector into doing exactly as Hades wished. That's also why I'm leaving tonight. The battle is near."

"You always had a way with your god-given magic," Allison shook her head, glaring at her twin. "But you brought me back to do what? If you already made a Soul Decree..."

"Only with half of it," Emma smirked. "Which means if I betray him, only that half of myself will die."

"Which half?" Allison asked, suppressing her rage at the answer she assumed was coming.

"My Olympian half," said Emma, with no trace of regret. "When the time comes, Aphrodite will be gone forever."

"Do you have any idea what an idiotic mistake you've made?" Allison snarled. "You gave up the divine!"

"Whatever we were, sis," Emma growled, "it was never divine. Besides, I wouldn't be calling anyone else stupid if I was wearing that outfit."

"Oh, don't even start," Allison clenched her fists.

"I never enjoyed being an Olympian," said Emma. "But I love being Emma Berggrias! And I also love my family, my twin sister! I preferred not to bring Athena back; that Olympian was a cruel bitch! But I did so because I need someone to protect Ellie and Dad while I'm gone!"

"Since when do you care about Dad?" Allison frowned. "I know, you've always loved Ellie, but... Ellie's Artemis, isn't she?"

"Yes," Emma forced the words out of her mouth. "And we both know how important it is she doesn't regain her godly self, either. So, protect them. I'll be back as soon as I can."

Emma turned towards the open bedroom window.

"How many of us are in Regal City?" Allison asked.

"Almost all of us," Emma sighed, "but none have been revived yet."

Emma started climbing out of the window as Allison spoke one last time, "I'll miss you."

"No, you'll miss Aphrodite," said Emma darkly as she held back a tear, "just like I'll miss my sister."

"AMELIA HAS OPENED A portal to hell," Hades said plainly.

"So, what?" Emma glared at him. "You and Hec can stop that easily after you revive him."

"Only if you give me what is needed," Hades smirked. "And you know what that is."

"Yes," Emma snarled, "I do. Every dark ritual needs a supernatural sacrifice."

"Yes, indeed," Hades chuckled. "Tell me, Aphrodite, ... which one of our siblings will die tonight?"

"...The one who deserves it the most," Emma said calmly.

"YOU CALLED, MOTHER?"

Emma was standing outside the Hoof. It was time for an official reunion of sorts. Tristan stood before her and his expression was anxious. All of his grand bravado, completely lost at the thought of being reunited with the woman who raised him.

"Tristan," Emma gave a watery smile. She didn't think it would hurt this much to see him again, knowing the part of herself that remembered him would be gone if they were successful.

His eyes widened in disbelief. "You really have returned!"

Emma hugged Tristan lovingly. "You've grown up to be the warrior I always knew you could be."

Tristan wiped his own tears from his face as he smiled. "You don't know how much I missed you and Father."

"I can imagine," Emma gave a small chuckle. "I will say, though, that you kept some shitty company while we were gone."

"That's the first time I ever heard you curse," said Tristan, shaking his head. "I never thought I would see the day, to be honest. You always loathed crassness."

"Things change, Tristan," Emma sighed. "Even immortals. I just wish I had more time to show you how much."

"Never fear, Mother," said Tristan, "once we defeat Hades, our family will have all the time in the world."

"...You're right," Emma tried to give the most sincere smile she could. "Did you bring the Amarus Orb?"

"Yes, I was able to steal it from Legend's facility without anyone even noticing," said Tristan. "But I don't know why you would want it. The Dragon Master it sired, had already drained all the magic out. It's nothing more than a mere paperweight now."

"Tristan, you should have already learned," Emma sighed, "nothing is ever as it seems."

Tristan handed the orb to Emma, who pocketed it quickly. "Stay on task, Tristan, and hidden when not. I love you. You are the greatest accomplishment that your father and I ever made. But I have to go now if we're going to succeed. Hades is expecting me. I'll be in touch with you as soon as I can."

"EMMA... WHY ARE YOU... doing this?"

Henry Wheeler was lying in a pool of ichor. Emma glared at him in disgust. She had already used her Deicide to amputate his arms and legs. Truth be told, she had enjoyed hearing his shrieks of pain and terror. The poor bastard really didn't remember who he used to be... what hell he had put her through. Emma hated to even remember the horrors of her past that he — Hephaestus — had caused!

"...Because you're the one who deserves it," Emma growled. She stabbed one of her Deicide daggers into his chest and pinned him against the alley wall next to CK. "I can't risk you letting Tristan know or Arnold remembering the truth. No one can know but me!"

Emma swung her other Deicide dagger swiftly as Henry's head fell off and splashed in the golden ichor.

Emma knew this had to end. She couldn't let the darkness, the insanity, or the sheer fury of Aphrodite ever consume her again. It was time for the Olympians to finally fade away. They were exiled from heaven for a reason. Emma's siblings would call that a curse. She didn't. No. This was her second chance.

"WELCOME HOME, APHRODITE," Hades gave her a deep bow.

"Cut the crap," Emma rolled her eyes. "I'm only here because I have to be. Now, who in the hell is so important for me to meet at three in the freaking morning?"

"Everyone," Hades smirked.

He gestured her into a large training room that resembled a Grecian temple. Inside was a young Fae girl with electric-pink hair casting attack spells at a tall, tan, blonde knight, along with a guy summoning metal to his hands and making it liquify onto his body, and a buff soldier firing off Quantum Gauntlets at three innocent, mortal, captives.

Emma looked at Hades in surprise. "Who are these people?"

"I told you earlier," Hades smirked widened, "the only mortal standing in our way is a young man named Jason Gardner. And these people are everyone he and his friends have lost over the years. Just decked out in new, more stylish attire."

"That's sick," Emma fumed. "Even for you!"

"No, it is love, dear sister," Hades laughed. "Our gift to the mortals who will serve us. Just in a darker form. You, out of all of us, should remember that. If not, you had better get reacquainted with it quickly. Because this is just the beginning!"

The End?

Did you love *Olympus Rising*? Then you should read *The War Of The Beast Trilogy* by Robert G. Culp!

When an ancient evil rises...

...six misfits must rally together.

But has their destiny already been written?

Two teenage star-crossed lovers formed a team who would become their family. They thought their future was bright, but a war is fast approaching. The fate of all reality hanging in the balance.

To succeed, they must uncover the true reason why Camelot fell.

What no one could predict was their bond would unleash a hellish end.

Can destiny be rewritten by love and loss?

You'll love this incredible YA Urban Fantasy Trilogy because it has the perfect mix of magic, thrills, adventure, and romance to keep you turning the pages.

Read more at https://robertgculp.com/.

About the Author

Robert G. Culp was born in the small town of Stuttgart, Arkansas and is the author of *The Mystic Brat Journals*, a series of three titles with a fourth in progress. The books follow students at a top secret government school, where teenagers are taught to fight the mythical, mystical, and cursed dangers that surround the world. His standalone short story, *Mirrorville*, is also set within the same continuity.

In his free time Robert enjoys watching TV shows and films, reading Urban Fantasy books, comic books and online fanfiction, while researching Greek mythology, supernatural legends and Arthurian lore.

His greatest achievement is to make his readers happy and entertain them with a few pages of pure escapism.

Read more at https://robertgculp.com/.